The Straits of Mystery

by G. H. Teed

From the Union Jack magazine,
Series 22, No. 1049, 17 November 1923

Illustrated by Eric Parker

Stillwoods Edition

Stillwoods.Blogspot.Ca

Catalogue Information:
Title: The Straits of Mystery
Author: G. H. Teed
First published in the Union Jack magazine, Series 22, No. 1049, 17 November 1923
Illustrated by: Eric Parker
This Edition by: Stillwoods, 2021
ISBN Canada: 978-1-989788-44-8
Blog: Stillwoods.Blogspot.Ca
Author Blog: http://ghteed.blogspot.com/
Storefront: http://www.lulu.com/spotlight/lulubook22

A comprehensive live list of the stories of G. H. Teed is online:
https://www.dropbox.com/s/s42sacikcdzujjl/Teed%20Index%20Latest.xls?dl=0

Keywords: Sexton Blake, British fictional detective, Tinker, George Marsden Plummer.

Cautionary Note: This series of books by Stillwoods are intended to make the stories of G. H. Teed, born in New Brunswick, Canada, available to collectors and researchers. The editor, or rather digitizer has not altered the original publication.

This story may contain language and racial terms that are not appropriate to today. I apologize for them; I know that the author was using his voice to excite and entertain an adventurous English audience. These works were published from 82 to 110 years ago. Most every work has characters of redeeming ethnicity within.

I hope you enjoy and share these stories; I have.
Doug Frizzle

The STRAITS OF MYSTERY

Not many people know that there is a very remarkable legend in connection with the Straits of Gibraltar. There is supposed to be a tunnel connecting the Rock of Gibraltar with Tangier, in Africa, on the opposite shore. The author of this brilliant story makes use of that legend as the background of another encounter between George Marsden Plummer, the ex-Scotland Yard man turned crook, and Sexton Blake. You will certainly enjoy this yarn to the last line, but before you plunge into it, it would be as well to read the author's note on page 7.

A Long Complete Story of Mystery and Adventure, featuring GEORGE MARSDEN PLUMMER and SEXTON BLAKE.
    SEXTON BLAKE and TINKER in GIBRALTAR!

Not many people know that there is a very remarkable legend in connection with the Straits of Gibraltar. There is supposed to be a tunnel connecting the Rock of Gibraltar with Tangier, in Africa, on the opposite shore. The author of this brilliant story makes use of that legend as the background of another encounter between George Marsden Plummer, the ex-Scotland Yard man turned crook, and Sexton Blake. You will certainly enjoy this yarn to the last line, but before you plunge into it, it would be as well to read the author's note.

THE MYSTERY of the STRAITS.
    It is stated by some prominent geologists and several officials who have been stationed at Gibraltar that one or more subterranean passages exist beneath the Straits of Gibraltar, and connect the Rock with Tangier in Morocco.
    Several curious incidents have occurred at different times of which there is authentic record to support this theory. There are those who even go so far as to say that these passages were known to and made use of, by the great Carthaginian conqueror, Hannibal, who certainly landed in Spain in very mysterious fashion and devastated the whole country, even crossing the Pyrenees and marching along the south coast of Gaul before Rome even guessed that he was in Europe.
    Some fifty years ago a British officer, who was stationed at the Rock at the time, paid a visit to Tangier, on the southern side of the Straits.
    While in Tangier he wandered into the deepest part of the bazaar, where he came upon the ruins of what was unquestionably an ancient Carthaginian temple. In poking about the place he stumbled upon an opening which led underground, and which he followed for some distance; but, owing to the fact that he had no light, and that several other confusing passages opened up, he desisted and returned to the outer air.
    This officer had heard the legend, and had made some study of it, but had been unable to prove anything definite. On this occasion,

however, as he emerged into the courtyard of the ancient ruins, he came upon a small monkey, such as are found only in Morocco and on the Rock. The presence of these monkeys on the Rock has often been quoted as proof that an undersea way did exist, but others have explained it more simply as being due to their having been originally brought across by the Moors, or even earlier invaders of Spain.

This officer managed to entice the little monkey into his hands, and, having picked up a cheap silver chain in the bazaar on his way through, he tied the chain about the neck of the monkey. Then he let it go, and watched it as it disappeared into the underground opening from which he had just emerged.

Shortly after that the officer in question was transferred to the East; but some two years later a British soldier stationed on the Rock caught a small monkey up near the top which he wanted as a pet. And about the monkey's neck he found a tarnished silver chain, such as one might buy in the Tangier bazaar. It is, of course, quite possible that the monkey had at some time previously been someone's pet, and that its master had tied the chain about its neck. But the coincidence, coming only two years after the officer's experiment in Tangier, is worth recording.

The author is not prepared to state categorically that there is a passage under the sea between the Rock and Tangier, but if such does exist, it has been originally the work of Nature, and not of man, and certainly many other very curious incidents could be quoted which would seem to admit of no other explanation.

And, too, one must remember that at no very distant date, geologically speaking, the Rock and Tangier were connected, and that when the great upheaval came, and the Atlantic burst through, the almost unimaginably terrific swirl of the waters must have cut a multitude of channels and tunnels before earth and sea became quiescent once more.—AUTHOR.

The BINDABLE Supplement.

Owing to unavoidable pressure on space it has not been possible to publish the regular 5-page Supplement this week. Those who wish to bind their Supplements into book form should cut pages 17 and 18 at the edge of the opposite column. Entrants for the Footballers' Names contest will also find that they can participate without mutilating the Sexton Blake story. Volume One of the Supplement will be complete with the December 29th issue. The New Year will start a new and improved volume. Save your copies—they're worth binding!

Note: My digital PDF file does not include any supplementary material. /drf

THE Libby liner Blankshire, homeward bound from Rangoon and Colombo, had had the smoothest passage her captain had experienced for years.

It had been hot in the Bay of Bengal, but smooth, and as the Blankshire was well equipped with electric fans, and had her own ice-making plant, the passengers felt little inconvenience.

After leaving Colombo it had been a race across the top part of the Indian Ocean and the Arabian Sea to beat the monsoon, which Captain Nelson knew was even then beginning to sweep across from the east coast of Africa. They had just made it, and, with the exception of a "flick of the tail" off the island of Socotra, they had seen nothing of the deluge. From that it had been delightful—cool and limpid waters at Aden, not too hot in the Red Sea, and calm as a millpond crossing from Port Said to Marseilles.

In fact, so pleasant had it been on the Mediterranean that numerous passengers, who had intended originally disembarking at Marseilles to make the overland crossing to London, decided to remain on board and make the circuit through the Straits of Gibraltar and up through the Bay of Biscay. It meant about a week longer, but, if one wasn't pressed for time, it loomed more pleasantly than the stuffy train journey from Marseilles to Paris, and thence to Calais for the Channel crossing.

Besides that, the captain had let it be known that, contrary to the usual schedule of the Libby Line, the Blankshire would remain at the Rock for some twelve hours, and as they were due to arrive there about ten in the morning, it meant that those who wished to go ashore and explore the famous fortress would have the whole day to do it in.

At Marseilles nearly a score of English passengers had come aboard. It is extraordinary how small is the number of persons who take advantage of the round trip which one can make from London or Liverpool and return by crossing to France and proceeding by train to Marseilles, where one can join one of the numerous homeward-bound liners for the sea voyage of eight days or so. Most of the lines running to and from the Far East make quite a feature of this, and it is becoming more and more popular each year with those who have been spending a holiday on the Riviera.

Among the score or so who embarked at Marseilles for the sea trip was a tall, broad-shouldered, lean-framed gentleman, who was evidently well known to the officers of the Blankshire, for on his appearance he was hailed most cordially by the chief officer; and, a little later, when Captain Nelson appeared, his face lit up with pleasure on seeing him. With this gentleman was a young man of sturdy build who seemed equally well known on board, and who was received with open arms by the two junior officers, "sparks," and the two apprentices.

And their identity soon became known to those standing about at the time, for the captain addressed the newcomer by name.

"Well, Mr. Blake, this is pleasant to have you for the run home with us. I hope you have been well since we last had the pleasure of carrying you out to Ceylon with us. And how are things going with you, my lad? You are certainly filling out— eh, what?"

Both Sexton Blake and Tinker smiled, for it was quite true that the lad had been developing astonishingly during the past year or so.

"We were in Marseilles on business, and I thought it would be pleasant to run home by sea, especially when I discovered the Blankshire was due to-day. Have you had a good run?"

"Splendid! Can't remember a better in twenty years. Sea like a millpond the whole way—missed the monsoon by twenty-four hours. You will sit at my table, Mr. Blake? A few passengers have left, and I believe there are two or three vacant places there."

"Thank you, captain, we shall be pleased. What is this I hear about a stop at the Rock?"

"That's right. Got a Government bigwig on board, who has some sort of inspection to make at Gib. Got orders from London to put him ashore and wait for him. Take about twelve hours. Arrive in the morning. Give the passengers all day to spend ashore. Must hurry away now, Mr. Blake. See you at tiffin. Don't forget—my table."

With that the affable skipper bustled off, and Sexton Blake and Tinker went below to superintend the stowing of their luggage, which, as they were travelling fairly light, did not take long. Then they returned to the deck, where Blake got hold of the deck steward, and arranged for their chairs to be placed on the starboard side, so that they could have the benefit of the view of the Spanish coast and the lovely Sierras on the way down to the Straits.

That arranged, they idled about the deck, watching the bustling scene on the dock, and forward, where the second-officer was superintending the loading of cargo for London. They were still thus pleasantly engaged, when the bugle for tiffin sounded, and after a few minutes they descended. Apparently the captain had found time to speak to the chief steward about their places, for, after greeting them, he led them at once to the captain's table.

Both Blake and Tinker bowed formally to the other passengers at the table, and it was soon evident that the rumour had gone round that Sexton Blake, the famous criminologist, was on board, for it wasn't long before the neighbour on Blake's left—an American millionaire from the Middle West, as Blake discovered a few minutes later—put the question to him bluntly.

Blake acknowledged the accusation with a smile, and on that the millionaire took it upon himself to introduce Blake and Tinker to the other passengers at the table. From what was said, it appeared that most of them were in the millionaire's party, and it wasn't long before Blake found that they were just completing a tour of the world.

While he listened to the American's relation of the five months' tour, Blake quietly sized up the various members of the party.

There was the millionaire's wife, a stout lady, whose fair hair looked to Blake as if a good deal of peroxide had been expended on it. There was a young lady of about eighteen summers, the millionaire's daughter, a delightfully friendly girl, whom both Blake and Tinker liked at once. There were two young men who had been vaguely introduced as secretaries, and a dark-skinned young man of Egyptian cast of countenance, who had been introduced as Prince Ben Ali Said, and who, the millionaire confided to Blake, had joined them at Colombo as courier, to conduct them about the different points at which they would touch between there and London.

Blake knew the type well enough, which is sufficient to say that he considered him an undesirable person either socially, or in the role of courier, although, of course, he gave no hint of his feelings to the American.

The captain appeared presently, and a few minutes later they felt the throb of the screw as the big liner began to steam slowly down the basin on her way out to sea. From that point the conversation became general, although neither the two secretaries nor the Egyptian courier took much part in it.

Most of the attention was centred on the captain's end of the table, for that affable sea dog was regaling Mrs. MacFarlane, the wife of the millionaire, with some highly-coloured tales of the doings of Sexton Blake, much to that gentleman's outward amusement and inward confusion. As for Tinker, he was enjoying it all hugely, and when Nancy MacFarlane, the daughter, began to question him, it must be regretfully said that he proved an able second to the captain.

They were all rather a friendly lot on board—which can't always be said of a bunch of passengers after a long voyage —and the run down past the coast of Spain proved quite as enjoyable as it had been at Port Said. They passed the wonderful snow-capped Sierras and the Balearics, ran past Barcelona without seeing it, but encountered several vessels bound to or from that busy port; then, in a sea like glass, they rounded the angle of Spain, and steamed along towards the Straits.

The Blankshire was running true to time, for it was almost exactly ten o'clock in the morning when she came to anchor off Gibraltar, and there was an immediate bustle on board by those who had decided to spend the day ashore. Among these were Sexton Blake and Tinker, and since the American millionaire had been kind enough to invite them to join his party, they had accepted.

Mr. MacFarlane had wirelessed for a large private motor-launch, into which they all stepped, and as they sped towards the shore, with a warm sun overhead and a fresh breeze sweeping in from the Atlantic, little did any of them dream that stark tragedy lay ahead of them.

As Tinker was speaking to the girl a pair of black arms shot out of the opening by which he was standing and dragged him back out of sight. Before Nancy Macfarlane could cry out Prince Ben Ali Said was upon her. (*Chapter 2.*)

THE launch ran across the harbour to the Bland Company's jetty, where the party disembarked. As they had the whole day before them, it was decided that they should spend the morning in the lower town among the bazaars, and take lunch at the Victoria Hotel. After lunch, it was arranged that they should ride up to the peak, from which a view of the harbour and the Moroccan coast, as well as a magnificent panorama of the Spanish coast, could be obtained.

Sexton Blake and Tinker had both noticed on the way down from Marseilles that one of the young American secretaries and Prince Ben Ali Said were keen competitors for the favours of Nancy MacFarlane, and after a couple of days Tinker, too, had taken a hand in the game, more to plague the other two than anything else. In the launch, it had been obvious to him that both young men were endeavouring to manoeuvre so that they might have the privilege of escorting the girl through the bazaar; but, to their chagrin, the girl elected to accept Tinker's offer, explaining naively that since he had been on the Rock before and they hadn't he would be ever so much more useful in explaining things.

Tinker had felt an angry thrill run through him at the expression that had come into the Egyptian's eyes as the girl refused. He had promptly reminded her that he knew the Rock well, and that as a courier he was better qualified to be her guide than anyone else, but the girl had most effectually cut him short by reminding him coldly that, as courier, he had been engaged by her father, and she preferred him to that gentleman for his instructions.

The American youth had taken his "turn down" in good grace, and he grinned openly at the discomfiture of the Egyptian, and, while Tinker, too, had appreciated the neatness with which Nancy MacFarlane had handled the fellow, he again felt an angry surge as the same expression returned to the dark eyes of the Egyptian.

From that moment he resolved that he would stick close to Nancy MacFarlane the whole day in order to protect her from any further importuning on the part of the fellow. He wouldn't have felt the least bit offended if she had chosen the young American as her escort, for Tinker liked him, and knew that he was deeply in love with the girl, while as for himself it must be confessed that he was simply trifling along to pass the time away.

Thus it came, when they landed on the jetty that Prince Ben Ali

Said was manoeuvred along until he found himself beside Mrs. MacFarlane and the other secretary, while Caleb MacFarlane and Sexton Blake were ahead, with Tinker, Nancy MacFarlane and the other secretary—she had relented in his case at the last moment—behind.

They moved along leisurely to the shops, jostling their way through the medley of Greeks and Spaniards, Moors and Levantines, French and Italians, and Heaven knows what not that go to make up the population of the Rock. Now and then they glimpsed the countenance of a British soldier, who would glance at them in a friendly way, but for the most part the lower town was a smelling jumble of dark-skinned races, who seemed to be under the impression that no single thing in life could be accomplished without the accompaniment of high-pitched yells and cries.

Blake and Tinker, who had been at Gib. several times before, found the bazaars boring enough, for they compared very poorly with those of the East or of Tangier and Algiers. But, as it was a pleasant novelty for the two ladies, they hid their private opinions, and proved far more efficient as guides than Prince Ben Ali Said, who was supposed to know the place so well. In fact, during the morning, when they were seated outside a little cafe taking a rest and imbibing a cooling drink, Caleb MacFarlane confided to Blake his regret that he hadn't got rid of the fellow at Port Said.

"Don't know why I ever took him on," he grumbled. "Didn't want a courier any more than a cat wants nine tails. Came to me at G.O.H. and said he had heard from someone I wanted a courier for Egypt. At that time I half intended to get off at Port Said and do Egypt, but changed my mind, and didn't like to sack the fellow. Said he wanted to get to London, if possible, where he could get a party to take out to Egypt."

"Rather a curious time to take a party to Egypt," remarked Blake. "It is about the most 'off' season in that country. People don't go there in the summer."

"Sure. I mentioned that, but he said it was a scientific party he had in mind. But he's no good, I'll tell the world. But it doesn't matter. The missus likes to trot him round the deck and call him prince, so if it amuses her what's the odds?" And the millionaire grinned at some secret thought.

They finally reached the Victoria Hotel laden with parcels of bazaar rubbish which they had picked up during the morning. Prince Ben Ali Said proved himself useful for once by getting the whole lot of stuff sent down to the launch, and by managing to secure a cool spot on the terrace, where they had a fairly passable tiffin. After lunch the ladies retired for a brief rest, for the sun had grown very hot. While the male members of the party sought a shady spot in the garden to smoke, all except Prince Ben Ali Said, who asked his employer to excuse him while he went away to make arrangements for their journey up to the peak.

Sexton Blake was by no means averse to going up; for, apart from the wonderful defence galleries with which the British military engineers have honeycombed the great rock, he liked the view from the top more than anything else about Gib. It is bare and unattractive enough in the stony waste there, but the view is worth the effort, and, in addition, Blake had always been greatly fascinated by the hundreds of holes and openings in the stone, about which he had heard and read so much.

He whiled away the time by giving the millionaire an outline of the legend which had grown up about the subterranean passage connecting the rock with Tangier, a thing MacFarlane had never heard before. He was vastly interested, and asked many acute questions, which Blake did his best to answer.

It was supposed, so Blake explained, that some one of those hundreds of pits or holes on the top of the Rock gave access to the gallery which would lead to the undersea tunnel, but added that, although men had searched for it for years, it had never been found, and that more than a few persons had disappeared while searching, never to be heard of again.

From this the conversation went back to ancient times, and they were idly speculating whether Hannibal really did know of such a tunnel, and if, knowing of it, he did bring his army across that way, when Prince Ben Ali Said returned to say that he had arranged for donkeys for the trip up the hill. The millionaire went off to inform his wife and daughter and pay the score, and about a quarter of an hour later they got started.

If one takes a donkey and doesn't mind the short gait of the animal it isn't such a bad journey up to the top of the Rock, and on this occasion Mrs. MacFarlane was the only one who made any complaint, although Tinker whispered to Blake that he had more sympathy for the donkey than for the lady. They were held up once by a British sentry, who passed them after a brief scrutiny, then they continued the winding way until the harbour and the lower town seemed far, far beneath them.

But they had still some way to go before they should get the full glory of the wonderful view, and as the way became rougher it was only natural that they should become separated at times.

Tinker, who was fully alive to the possibilities of the situation, soon discovered that the Egyptian was making subtle efforts to get himself close to Nancy MacFarlane, so Tinker at once made an effort to outwit him. He jostled his way along until he was close behind the girl, and there he held his animal despite the sneer on the face of the Egyptian.

Blake was in the lead, and as he reached the summit and rode along over the rocky ground beneath gaunt, dusty-leaved trees, he pointed out the occasional glimpse one got of the Spanish coast. He also discoursed to the millionaire about the gaping holes which seemed to honeycomb the ground in countless hundreds, and which formed miniature caves, some of which yawned in sinister gloom. Overhead dozens of the strange little monkeys found on the Rock swung from branch to branch, chattering angrily at the invaders, and on several occasions one could be seen to disappear into one of the dark openings. It was certainly a curious formation that, but it seemed scarcely possible that any one of those openings could follow a course from such a height to the sea bottom far beneath, and thence undersea across the Strait to the African shore, which was not plainly visible.

Blake drew up in an open space and all hands dismounted. They walked about a bit to stretch their legs, while one of the donkey boys opened a tea hamper. Blake began an impromptu lecture concerning the various points of interest, to which the millionaire and his wife listened with absorbed attention.

But Blake was not to have it all his own way as a guide, for Prince Ben Ali Said had evidently succeeded in getting Nancy MacFarlane into a softened mood after her brusqueness of the morning. He had been speaking to her in a low, pleading tone, Tinker had observed, and the lad saw the girl give a laugh and a shrug, and permit the prince to lead her off to one side to show her some view which he had apparently been dilating upon. Tinker, still determined to queer the other's pitch, followed after, and soon came up with them.

Prince Ben Ali Said glowered at him as he made a cheerful observation to Nancy MacFarlane, but there was a faint expression of relief in the girl's eyes at the sound of his voice, and that was sufficient to make Tinker determined to stick with them. The Egyptian seemed to accept the situation, for he began talking of the Rock, and became interesting even to Tinker when he dwelt at some length on the history of the place.

It was Tinker who asked Nancy MacFarlane if she had heard that there was a subterranean passage under the Straits. She assured him that she hadn't, and was all eagerness for him to tell her about such a romantic thing. Tinker nodded towards the Egyptian.

"I fancy the prince could tell you better," he said good-humouredly. "He seems to have the whole business at his finger-tips."

Both Tinker and the American girl were surprised at the violence with which the Egyptian said:

"That is all stuff and nonsense! There is no undersea passage! Someone has been building up a joke! No such thing has ever existed!"

"Well, don't get so touchy about it," grunted Tinker. "If you won't tell Miss MacFarlane about it I will. It's this way, Miss MacFarlane. It is supposed that when the Atlantic broke through here and formed the Mediterranean — some say that was when the Biblical flood occurred—the upheaval of sea and land made the passage which is now the Straits of Gibraltar, and—"

But that was the last word Tinker uttered on the subject, for at that moment a pair of black arms shot out of one of the openings beside which he was standing and dragged him back out of sight.

Before Nancy MacFarlane could cry out in her horror, Prince Ben Ali Said was upon her, and although she kicked and struggled and tried to scream, he choked off her cries and thrust her into the hole where Tinker had disappeared. He himself slid in after, and the only witnesses of the dastardly attack were the chattering monkeys in a tree outside.

The Third Chapter.   Sexton Blake is Anxious.

TEA had progressed for some little time before any concern was expressed at the absence of Nancy, Tinker, and Prince Ben Ali Said.

It was Mrs. MacFarlane who remarked that they should have returned, and, while Blake was a trifle surprised that Tinker should not be on time for such, in Tinker's opinion, an important function, he made some slight remark, and the conversation turned into other channels.

But by the time it was practically finished, and only a little lukewarm liquid remained in the thermos flasks for the absent ones, Mrs. MacFarlane was beginning to get a little uneasy, for, although, like a good many matrons, she performed some rather silly rites in order to make herself appear as young as she had been many years before, she was at heart a very devoted mother; and Nancy MacFarlane, being an only child, was very dear to both her and her husband.

In order to ease her mind, Blake offered to go and scout about, and the two secretaries at once volunteered to accompany him. The millionaire wanted to come too, but Blake insisted that Mrs. MacFarlane should not be left alone; so, after lighting cigarettes, the three set off. Blake, who spoke several dialects of Arabic fluently, paused to question the donkey boys as to which way the missing ones had gone; but, beyond a vague pointing in a general way, he elicited nothing from them. With a shrug he started on again, with the two young Americans on either side of him.

The general lie of that part of the Rock was a miniature tableland, very rough and stony, pitted with innumerable holes and caves, and dotted with the gaunt dusty-leafed trees through which the chattering monkeys played. It was very different from the well-shaded road along which the ladies of the fort took their afternoon drive into Spanish territory.

But Blake had been there often before, and he knew that it should not be difficult to locate the truants, as the whole flat space could be pretty well covered in half an hour. What did occur to him was that one of the trio may have fallen and sprained an ankle, but he reflected that if such was the case, it would be like Tinker to inform them at once, unless it was he who had suffered.

Not for a moment was Blake seriously perturbed. But by the time they had been wandering about for nearly half an hour, searching in every likely spot, poking their heads down holes and calling, a worried frown appeared on his brow. Even then no suspicion of foul play crossed Blake's mind. At the worst, he thought the adventurous youngsters, accompanied by the Egyptian, had started to explore one of the openings, and had, perhaps, got farther in than they had intended.

He now began to prosecute the search systematically. He sent one of the young Americans off to the right, and another off to the left, each a distance of some hundred yards or so. In this way they worked along in line, back and forth until their beats, if one may use the term, touched. Not a hole, not a cave, not a hollow was left unexplored, and, although they shouted lustily down many a sinister cavern, no reply came from the missing ones.

The two Americans were plainly showing acute anxiety, Blake, too, began to feel distinctly uneasy, but he gave no sign. He knew, however, that something was wrong somewhere; and he knew that it was not going to be easy to go back to the millionaire and his wife with no news of Nancy.

He lit a fresh cigarette, and, standing on a slight eminence, gazed off towards the purple line that marked the Moroccan shore. He was trying to figure out just what could have happened.

He recalled how Nancy had started off with Prince Ben Ali Said, and how Tinker had followed. He remembered then that he had noticed some of the byplay in the launch in the morning, but at the time he had given little thought to it, putting it down as usual enough among young folks.

But now he recalled how persistently Tinker had stuck beside Nancy all during the day, and he began to wonder if the lad had not been entirely mischievous when he had ambled off after the girl and the prince just before tea.

"It is deucedly strange," he mused. "Tinker has been here before, and he knows his way about. He knows the risks of climbing into one of these holes here. He is perfectly aware that a misstep might take one into a deep drop that would mean death. He knows, too, that those caves are swarming with scorpions. I know the lad well enough to be quite sure that he would never permit a girl to enter one of them. Yet they are not to be found, and they couldn't have started down the hill unless we had seen them. Now, just what the deuce is the meaning of it all?"

Blake tossed his cigarette away and rejoined the two young Americans.

"I don't know why they haven't come back," he said curtly. "They may be playing a practical joke on us, but it is getting late, and we shall have to smoke them out. You two go along and whip up the donkey boys. I will speak to Mr. MacFarlane, and we shall make a systematic search of the whole place."

With that he led the way back to where the millionaire and his wife were seated. Both were distinctly worried now, and, no matter how carefully Blake chose his words, he could not deny the straight question which Mrs. MacFarlane shot at him.

In the meantime, the other two had dug out the donkey boy, and were ready to begin the search. Blake marshalled everyone in line, even the millionaire and his wife insisting on taking part, and, in this way, they began to cover every foot of the little plateau. For a solid hour they worked back and forth, searching and calling, but only the echoes of their own voices, and the excited screaming of the monkeys, answered them.

When they had gone over every possible part where the missing ones might be found, and had no result, Mrs. MacFarlane began to grow hysterical. She collapsed into tears, and, leaving her husband to soothe her, Blake called the two young men aside.

"I am going to be frank with you," he said quietly. "I don't like things at all. They are certainly not in sight or in hearing. The only possibility I can think of is that they have entered one of the openings and have tried to penetrate it. They may have gone farther than they intended, and may have found it impossible to get back. At any rate, the thing is serious. If they have to spend the night in there, it will be a very unpleasant thing.

"This is what I propose doing. I have some acquaintance with the governor of the Rock. I want you two to remain here and continue the search. I shall persuade Mr. and Mrs. MacFarlane to come down to the hotel with me, and I shall then get in touch at once with the governor. I shall ask him to give me some men, a regiment if necessary, and some lights, and we shall make a thorough search of every hole on this plateau."

The two American youths, who had an immense respect for Sexton Blake, were duly impressed at his words. They quickly agreed to do as he suggested, and then all three made their way back to where

Caleb MacFarlane and his wife were waiting.

It was not an easy thing that Blake had to perform just then. He was growing more and more uneasy at the continued absence of the three missing ones, and he was probably the only one there who realised exactly how grave the position would be if, as he was beginning to believe, the trio had entered one of the pits.

He made a private note that he would give Tinker a jolly severe wigging for embarking upon such a foolhardy stunt as soon as he should get his hands on that young man, but in the meantime there was only one thing to do, and Blake knew operations would have to be begun without delay.

Not for a single moment did he think that the absence of Tinker and Nancy was not of a voluntary nature.

Mrs. MacFarlane was inclined to become hysterical as Blake tried to put things before them, but Caleb MacFarlane was a man quick on the uptake, and he soon realised that Blake's plan was the wisest. He took his wife in hand while Blake went to summon the donkey boys, and a few minutes later they started back for the hotel.

As soon as they reached the Victoria Caleb MacFarlane secured a suite for his wife, while Blake went off to try and get an interview with the governor. There was some delay before he finally managed to get his card through to his Excellency, but after that things moved more swiftly.

In a few words Blake explained what had happened, and followed this by his request for some soldiers to help prosecute the search. The governor nodded his head.

"Certainly, Mr. Blake, I will give you as many men as you need, but frankly, between ourselves, I don't like the situation. From time to time a soldier is reported missing at that spot, and, although on each occasion a thorough search has been made, not once has the missing man been found.

"My own opinion is that they have foolishly tried to penetrate one of the holes, and have fallen over a cliff or ledge. No one knows exactly what is down there except the monkeys. But I will do as you wish. I am sorry I did not know you were on the Rock. I should have been delighted to have you lunch with me!"

"I am just travelling round by sea from Marseilles." said Blake. "I came ashore with the American party, and as I understood someone from Government was engaged with your Excellency, I did not come to Government House to pay my respects. I shall be most grateful to your Excellency for some men and, if possible, some naphtha flares, in case we have to continue the search after dark."

"I shall give orders at once for everything you will need. And I wish you would keep me informed how the search progresses. I shall be anxious to hear that the young lady has been found safe. And, needless to say, the pleasant lad who is your assistant."

Blake again thanked the governor warmly, and hurried back to the hotel to inform the MacFarlanes that some soldiers were being sent out on the search.

He had some difficulty in persuading Caleb MacFarlane to remain at the hotel, but as Mrs. MacFarlane was beginning to grow more and more "nervy" he finally convinced him that his immediate duty was with her.

"You can rest assured that everything possible will be done to locate them before dark," said Blake reassuringly. "I myself shall take charge—and remember I am just as anxious about my lad, Tinker. Besides, if we cannot get back by the time the Blankshire is due to sail, it means we shall have to stay over, and it will need someone here to send out word for our luggage to be put ashore. If I know you are down here to attend to that, I can give my whole attention to the search."

At last he got away, and, needless to say, Blake lost no time in getting back to the peak. He cast many anxious glances towards the west, where, beyond the Spanish shore, the sun was dipping towards the rim of the Atlantic, for he knew how handicapped they would be after dark had fallen, despite the aid of the naphtha flares.

On reaching the peak he found that the governor had been as good as his word, for a hundred soldiers were already on the ground, in charge of three young officers, who were directing matters in a very efficient manner. They had been on that same job before, and they knew exactly what was to be done in order not to waste time.

The two young Americans had been searching diligently ever since Blake's departure, but reported that they had found not a single sign of the missing ones. Blake tried to keep his uneasiness down, but as each minute passed he grew more and more convinced that something far more serious than he had at first thought had overtaken the girl and the lad.

Somehow the thought of the Egyptian scarcely entered his mind, but possibly that was because there was no love lost between Sexton Blake and that race. In Cairo more than one determined attempt had been made to kill Blake; but, of course, he did not know whether Prince Ben Ali Said was one of the seditionists or not. He simply disliked him for the simple reason that he had met scarcely a single Egyptian whom he had found anything else but undesirable.

The three young officers soon had their men thrown out in a line that must eventually cover every foot of the miniature plateau, and, joining the line, Blake and the two Americans kept pace in the search until the sun dropped below the horizon and the sky in the east began to grow violet. At that point the powerful naphtha flares were prepared, and when the last streaks of rose died in the western sky they were lighted, and each flare was placed in charge of two men, to be carried at regular intervals along the line, so the search could be prosecuted almost as well as with broad daylight.

It was a strange scene that, on top of the greatest natural fortress in the world, with more than a hundred men strung out in line, the dazzling naphtha flares lighting up their faces grotesquely, the twinkling illuminations of the Rock beneath them in terrace after terrace, until at the edge of the water came the great semicircle of shore lights, and beyond those the pin-point gleams of the ships lying at anchor in the harbour.

Away across the Straits could be seen the light house on the Moroccan coast; to the west was the long roll of the Atlantic, where the twinkling brilliance of a homeward-bound ship could be seen; and to the east the gentle bosom of the Mediterranean, with two ships far out, and the widening space between their lights showing that one was bound up the Spanish coast—probably for Barcelona or Marseilles—while the other was coming down to Gib. There are few more imposing views to be found anywhere in the world than the view from the top of the Rock on a clear night.

Hour, after hour went by without the faintest sign from the three missing ones. It was perfectly obvious to all the searchers by now that things were very grave indeed, and, in view of comrades they had lost in the past, the soldiers were beginning to whisper to each other that they would never be found. Even the monkeys were chattering in subdued tones, and there was a sinister feeling about everything that took all one's will power to shake off. Of all the searchers Blake and the three officers were the only ones to retain their sangfroid. The two

American youths had sunk into the depths of apprehension long since.

By ten o'clock about half the plateau had been covered, when Blake noticed a native in the livery of the Victoria Hotel enter the circle of light. He stood hesitating for a few moments, then, as he saw Blake, he came towards him. As he reached him he held out an envelope; and, tearing it open, Blake took out the folded sheet of paper it contained. He opened it, and in the light of one of the flares read:

"Please come to the hotel at once— very urgent.
(Signed) "CALEB MACFARLANE."

Blake stuffed the note in his pocket and quickly explained that Mr. MacFarlane had sent for him. Then he made a sign to the man from the hotel and started on his descent. He travelled as fast as conditions permitted, and on reaching the Victoria found the millionaire pacing up and down the terrace, evidently in a state of great agitation. As he caught sight of Blake he gave an exclamation and hurried forward. Grasping him by the arm, he said:

"Come here—over in this corner. There is no one there. I want you to read "something."

Without a word Blake obeyed. As they paused the millionaire pressed a folded piece of paper into his hand. Blake opened it, noticed that it was written on the letter heading of the Bhanghadi Hotel, in Tangier, then he read the contents. This is the amazing message which confronted him:

"To Caleb MacFarlane, Esq.—If you wish to save your daughter it will be necessary for you to leave the steamer by which you are travelling, and repair at once to the above hotel in Tangier. Your daughter is not on the Rock, but in Morocco. On your arrival at this hotel you will learn more."

That was all. No signature. But just beneath the name of the hotel was written, "Eight o'clock evening," and somehow Sexton Blake knew it was no attempt at a hoax. He knew that something very sinister was threatening Nancy MacFarlane, and he knew, too, in that moment that their only hope of saving her was to obey the injunction of the letter to the last detail.

Caleb Macfarlane was gaping at the fierce, hawk-like countenance of the stranger, whose black, forked beard added to the ferocity of his expression. But Sexton Blake had risen. He had seen those features before. (*Chapter 4.*)

"WHAT do you make of it?" asked the millionaire, rather hoarsely.

"Wait a minute!" returned Blake. "This wants some thinking over."

He walked to the edge of the terrace, and stood gazing out across the harbour towards the winking pin-point of light that marked the Moroccan shore. He was not asking himself if the anonymous communication was a hoax. He knew instinctively that it was not.

He was thinking back to the afternoon, when they had first discovered that Tinker, Nancy, and Prince Ben Ali Said were missing. And he was calculating just about how long it would take to cover the distance from the Rock to the African shore on foot. Assuming it were possible to imagine making the journey in that way.

"It seems too preposterous for belief," he muttered. And yet — and yet how else was it done? If this letter was actually written in Tangier then it must have been done. Of course, someone who had been in Tangier could have brought a few sheets of the Bhanghadi Hotel paper back with him. The note could have been written in Gibraltar, and delivered at the Victoria. In that case, the contents were a lie, and that meant the missing ones were not in Tangier, but still on the Rock.

On the other hand, it would have been quite impossible for them to descend from the plateau, either willingly or unwillingly, without being seen by some others of the party. There was only one way, in Blake's opinion, that they had disappeared from view, and that was by means of one of the confusing holes in the ground. And if that were the case, had they—did they? But there Blake finished the extraordinary suggestion with a shrug.

He walked back to where Caleb MacFarlane stood waiting.

"What have you done about the Blankshire, Mr. MacFarlane?" he asked.

"As soon as I found the search was likely to last until late I took a launch and ran out to the ship. I saw the captain, told him what had happened, and tried to persuade him to remain until the morning. But he had orders from London to sail the moment the Government official was ready, and that was to be at midnight. So I gave instructions for our stuff to be packed and brought ashore. I also took the liberty of having your things packed, but did not have it brought ashore. I did not know whether you would wish to remain over or not. Of course, it is out of the question for me or my wife to leave until Nancy is found."

Blake nodded.

"Just wait here a few moments," he said. "I want to send a note out to the ship. I am staying over, of course, till I get news of Tinker, and I want my luggage brought ashore."

He hurried into the hotel and scribbled a hasty note to Captain Nelson, asking him to have his luggage sent to the Victoria. This he despatched by one of the hotel servants, and then rejoined the millionaire, who was pacing up and down in a frenzy of anxiety. Blake took him by the arm and led him back to the secluded corner of the garden.

"Now, look here, sir!" he said courteously but firmly. "This business has got to be faced, and we have got to deal with it in the same logical way we would handle an affair that did not concern us directly. Are you agreed on that?"

"I don't quite follow you, Mr. Blake, but I will do anything—anything, you understand—to get my little girl back safe!"

"And I will do anything to get my lad Tinker back safe," added Blake. "Therefore, we should be able to work fast between us. Now, take this letter first. I do not think it is a hoax, but I do believe it to be deadly serious. If it speaks the truth in saying that the missing ones are at present in Tangier, then, preposterous as it may seem, I can only figure out one way how they have been taken there, and that is by a subterranean tunnel which must run across from the Rock to some point near Tangier.

"I told you of that legend to-day. As far as is generally known, it has remained nothing but a legend; but, if any surmise is correct, then it means that someone—someone with a more than ordinarily shrewd brain has discovered the route of the tunnel, and has made use of it to-day in order to kidnap your daughter."

"But why? What on earth do they want of my little girl?"

"Ransom is the most probable motive," answered Blake. "Don't forget, Mr. MacFarlane, that you are a very well-known man. Everyone who reads the papers in almost any language knows that you are very wealthy, and your movements have been advertised for weeks past. But if your daughter and my assistant were kidnapped this afternoon it couldn't have been done without the co-operation of someone in close personal touch with the movements of your party, in such close touch that he could, to a certain extent, control those movements at a given time and place."

"Good heavens! What do you mean, Mr. Blake?"

"Prince Ben Ali Said is also missing." remarked Blake quietly.

"And you think—"

"Merely a suggestion so far. But let us return to that letter. It is what we must deal with first. It states that if you wish to recover your daughter you must cross to Tangier and go to the Bhanghadi Hotel, where further instructions will be given you. Well, there is only one thing to do."

"You mean?"

"Go. And I shall go with you."

"But—but what of my poor wife?"

"She must remain here. I think I can arrange that she shall be invited to remain at Government House until we return. Your two secretaries can remain here at the hotel. Incidentally, it will be as well to send up word as soon as possible to call off the search. I shall also communicate with the governor. And then we shall have to get a launch to run us across the Straits to-night."

"But what does it mean?" gasped the bewildered millionaire.

"I don't know yet," answered Blake Then, grimly: "But before we leave Tangier I am going to find out!"

Blake's plan was followed. He despatched a letter to the governor at Government House, and inside half an hour a reply was received, enclosing a very cordial invitation for Mrs. MacFarlane to stay there. The millionaire had no little difficulty in persuading his wife that this was the only thing for her to do, for she was rapidly working herself into a state of frenzy through her anxiety over Nancy's absence. Eventually Blake had to be called in, and when he had talked to her for a time she finally consented to do as they wished.

While Caleb MacFarlane took her along to Government House, Blake sent word to the peak to call off the search, and then arranged for a powerful launch to run them across to Tangier that night. It was nearly one o'clock when they finally got away, and each carried just one suit-case, containing enough changes to see them through two or three days.

It was a calm night, almost without a breeze, and the run across was both speedy and pleasant. Now that he had done what he could for the American, Blake had time to think over Tinker's plight.

His reason told him that if Nancy MacFarlane had been kidnapped then the coup must have been planned some time before. He could not get out of his mind the suggestion that Ben Ali Said had, in some way, played the traitor, and yet, if this were so, then it looked as if a plot must have been in progress against MacFarlane for a considerable time. Prince Ben Ali Said had been engaged at Colombo. Had someone had designs against MacFarlane that far back? Of course, there would have been no difficulty for interested persons to keep close track of the millionaire's movements, for they were published in all the papers, and, in addition, his name would naturally appear in all published lists of the Blankshire's passengers.

On the other hand, if that were so, then how could the plotters have known that they could bring off the coup at a certain time and place on the Rock? As far as Blake was aware, even Captain Nelson himself had not known that the Blankshire would stop at the Rock until he had received his instructions at Marseilles. If the plot were conceived after that, then it stood to reason that Prince Ben Ali Said, if he were an accomplice, must have been "got at" in Marseilles. But one thing was certain. The situation was a most sinister one, and if Tinker and Nancy MacFarlane were taken back into the desert country of Morocco, beyond the political zones of the French and Spanish Governments, it was going to be a very serious problem to get them back.

Sexton Blake knew that at that time there was a great deal of unrest among the Riff tribesmen. Indeed, the news each day showed that they had been attacking the Spaniards beyond Tetuan with no little success; and Blake knew that Spanish reinforcements were even then being rushed forward from Ceuta and across the straits from Malaga. Once the missing ones disappeared into the confused welter, it might take months—ay, years—before they could be released.

But, above all, was the stupendous possibility that a subterranean tunnel actually did exist between the Rock and the African shore.

Some years before Blake had read about everything that had ever been written on the subject, even going so far as to study some ancient manuscripts in the national archives at Madrid which gave a detailed account of how the tunnel was probably formed by the terrific upheaval ages before, when the Atlantic had broken down the land barrier and had burst through to form what is now the

Mediterranean. That, he knew, was a geographical fact —as it was also fact that in those dim times, when titanic forces were at work, what is now the vast Sahara Desert was salt sea.

One of these manuscripts also purported to give a line indicating the course followed by the tunnel, and reckoned that, with windings and dips, it covered, approximately, sixteen miles.

But more than one British officer had tried to discover the passage by following that plan, yet with no success. Some daring spirits had even tried to penetrate several of the holes in the peak, but on each occasion they had either come to a blind end or to the edge of an impassable precipice beyond which was only a black eternity.

Blake knew, however, of the occasional disappearance of British soldiers on the peak; and he knew of the experiment tried by a British officer half a century or so ago when he tied a silver chain round a monkey's neck in the Tangier bazaar, and how, some two years later, a monkey with such a chain about its neck was caught on the peak at Gibraltar. And in those incidents he found food for thought, considering what had happened that very afternoon.

They reached Tangier at half-past two, and, on negotiating a passage through the medley of native craft that packed the harbour, they came to a stop at the Bland Shipping Company's jetty.

There were no motor-cars or cabs to be seen at that hour of the morning, but they managed to get hold of a native to carry their bags, and, since Blake knew the place well, they set off on foot for the Bhanghadi Hotel, which Blake knew to be in the French quarter.

They found a couple of porters on duty when they reached the place, and after some negotiation Blake succeeded in arranging for a couple of large rooms and a sitting-room overlooking the courtyard about which the hotel had been built. They went at once to their rooms, but sat down in the sitting-room for a cup of coffee before turning in.

All the way across neither of them had spoken, but as they sipped their coffee Caleb MacFarlane said:

"Well, Mr. Blake, we have done as the letter said. When do you think the next move will be made?"

"That is difficult to say," responded Blake slowly. "I have not the least doubt that the person, or persons, who are responsible for the anonymous letter are fully aware of our arrival in Tangier. They might make the next move this very night. On the other hand, they may think it wise to keep us in suspense for a day or two. The only thing for us to do is to sit tight and wait."

"It is not going to be easy. I am thinking of my poor wife and my little girl."

"I know," said Blake, with a sympathetic nod. "But you may depend on it, Mr. MacFarlane, that the moment I see the faintest sign of an opening for action I shall seize it."

At that moment there came a light tap-tapping on the door, which they scarcely heard owing to the buzz of the electric fan overhead. Blake had caught it, however, and as he shot a warning glance at the American he raised his voice and called in Arabic. "Enter!"

The door swung open slowly, revealing the tall figure of a man dressed in long garments of flowing white and with a wide white burnous thrown about his shoulders and head, barely permitting a view of his eyes. He stepped into the room, and closed the door. Then he bowed, and, straightening up, threw the burnous to one side.

Caleb MacFarlane was gaping at the fierce, hawk-like countenance of the stranger, whose black forked beard added to the cold ferocity of his expression. But Sexton Blake had risen, and was standing facing the swarthy visitor. He had seen those features and that forked beard before, and he knew that the intruder was none other than the notorious Sakr-el-Droog, or Hawk of the Peak, a powerful chieftain among the most turbulent of the Riff tribes of the interior, and the man who was responsible for the violence of the warfare then being carried on against the Spaniards.

Yes, he knew Sakr-el-Droog as the Hawk of the Peak, but he also knew that Sakr-el-Droog was none other than the one-time inspector at Scotland Yard who had taken to criminal ways, and who was in reality George Marsden Plummer.

And, knowing that, Blake began to see a little light in the mysterious disappearance of Nancy MacFarlane and Tinker.

SAKR-EL-DROOG had no eyes for the millionaire. His gaze was fixed on his old enemy, Blake; and after a few moments his teeth showed white against the black beard as he smiled.

"So the report I received was true," he said softly in Arabic. "I had heard that Sexton Blake was in the party of Mr. Caleb MacFarlane, but I did not think I should be so fortunate as to have the pleasure of seeing you in Tangier. And, by the same token, it has already been reported to me that a young Englishman was taken at the same time that we extended our hospitality to Miss MacFarlane. Is it possible that it was your assistant Tinker?"

"Your powers of intuition are marvellous." replied Blake coolly in the same language. "I haven't a doubt that Tinker is the young man you refer to. You say you have him and Miss MacFarlane in your power. You have sent for Mr. MacFarlane to come here to the Bhanghadi Hotel. Well, Plummer—or Sakr-el-Droog, if you prefer it—what is the next move? You are in the French zone at present, but I have an idea if the Spanish authorities guessed that you were in Tangier they would be deeply interested in your movements."

Plummer snapped his fingers.

"That for the Spanish authorities!" he said contemptuously. "Have you read the papers lately?"

"Yes."

"Then you will know that the Spaniards have their hands more than full. We beat them back from Guamara two days ago—cleaned up a whole battalion. Those were my own fighting devils who did that. We have them locked up in Alhucemas, and we shall keep them locked up there. This is no ordinary uprising of the Riffs. This is a definite drive of the forces of the new Riff Republic, and we shall keep it up until we have driven the Spaniards clean out of the Riff country. They will see what Sakr-el-Droog will do to them."

"All very interesting, no doubt," remarked Blake, as he dropped into his chair. "It seems that I recall a visit of yours to London not long ago, when you came as the head of the Riff mission. You were not as successful on that occasion as you hoped to be, if I remember rightly."[1]

Plummer's eyes flashed. Looking at him in his desert clothes, and

---

[1]   For an account of this duel between Blake and Plummer, see "U. J.," No. 1,041, Sept. 22nd, 1923.

with his beard forked after the fashion of the bashas of old, with his skin tanned by desert winds and sand, as dark as any of the wild tribes he had adopted as his own, it was difficult for even Blake to believe that he was talking to an Englishman. The very spirit of the desert seemed to have entered into Plummer, making him a different person.

And as for the American, he was utterly at a loss to understand the drift of the conversation that was taking place between the two men.

"Perhaps I was not entirely successful," admitted Plummer, also taking a seat; "but I achieved a good deal. I will grant that you spoiled my plans, but you are not going to upset matters this time. All the winning cards are in my hand, and I am going to play them. The first winning card is the possession of the person of Mr. Caleb MacFarlane's daughter. I have planned that for a long time, and, since you were there when the kidnapping occurred, you will know whether my plans succeeded or not."

"The first trick may be yours, but the game is not finished yet," said Blake. "But just what do you want of Mr. MacFarlane? Is it ransom? He has come here as you wished. Perhaps you will enlighten us?"

"Of Mr. MacFarlane I do want something, which he will give," replied Plummer. "Of you I want nothing. If you succeed in getting away from Tangier alive, you may count yourself lucky, Sexton Blake! As for that infernal brat of yours, I shall see that he goes so far into the desert as a recruit for the slave-market that you will never hear of him again!"

"You tried that once before, Plummer; but things went wrong, if you will remember."

"They won't go wrong this time!" snapped the adventurer. "As for what I want of Mr. MacFarlane, I will tell —him. You may listen if you wish."

With that Plummer turned, and fixed his hawk-like gaze on the millionaire.

"You will be wise to listen to me, Mr. MacFarlane," he said curtly in English. "If you doubt that I mean what I am going to say, you may ask Sexton Blake whether I am capable of carrying out my threats or promises, whichever you wish to term them.

"As you have already guessed, no doubt, your daughter is in my power. It is a bad plan for travelling millionaires to permit their every move to be recorded in the daily Press. I have been interested in the course of your travels ever since you left Shanghai some months ago, Mr. MacFarlane. For a plan I had in mind a millionaire was necessary, and it was also essential that he should have something to lose for which he would pay heavily to get back.

"Your daughter filled that requirement. It will do no harm to tell you now that it was I who arranged that Prince Ben Ali Said should approach you in Colombo. And, as I intended, you took him on as courier. There was a difficulty in making sure that you should land at Gibraltar. Of course, it could have been managed that your daughter be kidnapped in Marseilles, but Gibraltar was much better. If the Blankshire had not received instructions to stop at the Rock, then you would have found yourself detained in Marseilles through some 'accident,' Mr. MacFarlane. But there luck was with me, and my agent—Prince Ben Ali Said—did the rest. It was all quite simple.

"And now your daughter is quite safe behind the Riff lines. It lies entirely with you whether she remains safe and is eventually restored to you, or—"

And Sakr-el-Droog finished with a shrug.

"What—what do you want, you bandit?" asked the millionaire hoarsely.

"I will tell you in three words. One million dollars! Wait!" he continued, holding up a lean hand as the American would have spoken. "Listen to what I have to say!

"You must have heard of the Riff mission which visited Paris and London some months ago. The purpose of this mission was to secure moral, if not financial, support in those capitals for the Riff Republic, which is now in course of formation. And I am proud to say that the whole idea of a Riff Republic is mine.

"Your companion—Sexton Blake—can tell you more of that mission on another occasion. In some ways it was successful, and in some ways it was a failure. But it paved the way for a financial mission later, and that is where you come in, Mr. MacFarlane.

"If you have read the recent London papers, or extracts from them, you will have read a so-called 'Warning to Investors' which purported to have been sent broadcast by the Havas agency at the instigation of the Madrid Government. That 'warning' stated that the Government of the Riff Republic was endeavouring to market an issue of one million pounds in bonds, and added that no persons should invest in them, as the Riff Republic consisted only of a few scattered tribes who had not yielded to the dominion of Spain, and who would never be in a position to pay either the interest or the principal. We hold very different ideas about that, and the Spanish Government will see what the Riff Republic is before we have finished with it!

"But that is aside. The warning was sufficient to spoil any chances we had of floating the loan, and therefore you, as a financier, will realise that we had to have recourse to other means. And we need that money without delay, in order to prosecute our campaign against Spain. We hold the advantage now, and I am determined to drive them back from Alhucemas before they can rush reinforcements from Malaga. I will do to them just what we did to them two years ago at Melilia!

"And that is how it came that, in reading of your tour of the world, Mr. MacFarlane, I made up my mind that you would be the person to come to the assistance of the Riff Republic. As I have said, the first step was to get into our power someone near and dear to you.

"We have succeeded in doing that, and she is now beyond reach of either the French or Spanish. The next step was to negotiate with you. That is why I sent word for you to come across to Tangier and wait at this hotel. I originally intended that you should come out as far as Tetuan, but instead of sending a messenger here I decided to come myself. Time is precious.

"The offer I have to make is just this. In return for one million dollars in bonds of the Riff Republic you will hand me that sum of money in United States currency, or, alternatively, half the amount in cash and a letter of credit on New York for the balance, as we have arms and ammunition to pay for, and our need is urgent.

"You must understand that this uprising is no mere mutiny. It is a combined effort on the part of all the Riffs to achieve independence, and even now our agents are flying across the desert from village to village, preaching a holy war. Inside a fortnight I shall have a further hundred thousand determined and fanatical Moors behind me, and then the Spaniards will be swept into the sea! That is my offer! You will be wise to accept it without quibble!"

The American glanced towards Blake, but the latter was smoking stolidly and gazing straight ahead of him. Then he turned his glance back to Plummer.

"It won't do any good to tell you what I think of you!" he said at last.

"You planned well when you kidnapped my daughter! But, even if I were disposed to meet your demands, you must realise that I don't carry a million dollars round in my hip-pocket! And how do I know that you would send my daughter back to me —safe?"

"As for that, you don't know. You would have to take my word. Also, I am perfectly aware that you don't carry that sum of money about with you. But there is the cable. It will take you only a day or so to arrange the matter. And if you or your companion are entertaining any ideas of betraying me to either the French or Spanish authorities, you can dismiss them from your mind. My presence in Tangier to-night is known to many of the Moors, but my way is well guarded, and I shall go unhindered, as I came. By morning I shall be back in my camp at Guamara. As soon as I have your answer I shall go. If you refuse to meet my demands, then I give you my word that your daughter shall be sent to grace the harem of one of the Riff chiefs!"

"What shall I do, Mr. Blake?" asked the American in trembling tones. "What can I do but meet this bandit's demands?"

"You have your wife and your daughter to think of," said Blake slowly. "To put it bluntly, Mr. MacFarlane, I feel that this is an instance where you must decide yourself what you will do."

"But you—what about the lad?" asked the American.

Plummer smiled as Blake glanced up.

"That is another matter," said Blake slowly. "Our friend, who has turned Riffian (and as he was always a ruffian it needed only that changing of a letter) will not make any demand for a ransom from me. It simply remains to be seen whether he will be able to carry out his threat before I succeed in rescuing Tinker."

Plummer was still smiling.

"Don't fool yourself about that," he said airily. "The brat goes to the slave-market!"

"If he does, I'll wipe that smile off your face before I kill you!" responded Blake evenly.

"We shall see about that. But enough. What is your answer, Mr. MacFarlane? Does your daughter go to a Riff harem, or do you take up a million dollars in Riff Republican bonds? Come! I must be getting away, as I have a long ride before getting beyond the Spanish lines."

"I shall curse you with my dying breath," answered the millionaire. "But because I am helpless—because I must think of the sanity of my wife and the safety of my daughter, I accept. I shall take steps to-morrow to realise on certain securities in America, and will have the money transferred by cable. Does that satisfy you?"

"Decidedly! I thought you would see the wisdom of accepting. When it becomes known that such a shrewd financier as Caleb MacFarlane has invested in Riff bonds to the tune of a million dollars, I think we shall have no difficulty in disposing of the balance in the American market. I shall send a messenger here to-morrow night. If you have nothing definite by then, he will return the following night. But let me counsel you not to lose any time. And now I will be gone, and inform your daughter that she will probably be released in a few days."

With that Sakr-el-Droog rose, and, before sweeping his burnous across his turbanned head shot a jeering smile at Sexton Blake. Then he whirled and was gone.

Caleb MacFarlane was gazing in a tentative manner at Blake, but the latter had risen, and, with some muttered remark, was making for his room. He returned a few minutes later wearing his hat, and, with scarcely a glance in the direction of the millionaire, went out.

And had the American glanced into the street a little later, he would have seen the tall, white-clad figure striding off into the sinister Tangier night as if some urgent purpose were driving him.

As for the millionaire, he wrote out a telegram to his wife, informing her that Nancy was safe and would be released in a few days, after which he undressed, and tried to snatch a few hours' sleep, though he woke up many times, and each time he wondered what Sexton Blake was doing.

As the two Moors turned the corner of the tunnel Tinker hurled the smashed lantern full at the leader. It caught him in the abdomen, and he went down with a grunt. The other lifted his rifle and fired. (*Chapter 6.*)

The Sixth Chapter.   Tinker's Adventure by Lantern-Light.

WHEN first Tinker felt himself gripped from behind and dragged down into the hole by which he was standing, his natural instinct was to struggle and to cry out. He made a lusty effort to do both, but before he could give effect to either impulse a voluminous cloth of some sort was jerked about his head, and he had just time to see the silhouettes of Nancy MacFarlane and Prince Ali Said struggling above him when he was yanked down with stunning force against the ground.

Following that, he was twisted over on his face, and his arms were dragged behind him and secured by what he took to be a broad piece of cloth. He was still trying to shout a warning to Nancy, but so thickly had the cloth been wrapped about his head that it was as much as he could do to breathe, let alone give voice.

Tinker's first thought as he lay helpless was that they must have been attacked by bandits. But then he recalled that fleeting vision of the girl struggling in the hands of the Egyptian, and another explanation came to him.

"It is the work of that greasy traitor." he thought. "I never did cotton to him, and I never liked the way he looked at Miss McFarlane. I'll bet he cooked this up after we landed on the Rock this morning. But what the dickens does he expect to gain by it? He can't carry her off down from the peak. He would be seen for certain. And he can't hope to keep her hidden here in one of these holes, for as soon as we are missed the guv'nor is bound to have the whole place thoroughly searched.

"What can be his motive? Does he want to force her to marry him? Or is he going to try and hold up the millionaire for a bunch of money? If he tries that game he won't get very far with it, and he can bet his sweet young life that as soon as I get loose I'm going to give him one peach of a beating-up!"

Which goes to show how little Tinker realised what he was actually up against.

The touch of moving feet told him that several persons were close to him, and he was still puzzled as to what would be the next move, when he felt himself picked up bodily and carried along for a short distance. Here he seemed to be lowered some ten feet or so, for he felt himself passed down from one person to another, then for the second time he was dropped heavily to the ground.

He lay there waiting for what was to come next. He knew he would gain nothing by struggling, and he wanted to get a line on just what was going on, for he guessed that Nancy must be close to him. It never entered Tinker's mind that he had been brought along except through the accident of his being with Nancy and Prince Ben Ali Said at the time, which was true enough.

Presently he was dragged to his feet, and he felt his hands being untied. Then the cloth was unwound from his head, and he stood blinking at the strange .scene which presented itself.

Of the opening through which he had been dragged he could see nothing. Nor was there any sign of daylight. He appeared to be in a narrow, low-ceilinged passage, and about him were grouped half a dozen fierce, black-faced and black-bearded men in white garments, whom he knew well enough were Moors. Someone was still holding his wrists behind him, and as he shifted a little he felt them given a warning twist.

Then as he turned his head a little he caught sight of Nancy MacFarlane, and standing beside her, a sly grin on his evil countenance, was Prince Ben Ali Said. As Tinker looked into the girl's eyes he saw that, while the assault must have shaken her considerably, there was no fear there. Indeed, she smiled at him bravely.

"I don't know just what the game is, Miss Nancy," Tinker said evenly, "but it is obvious that the greasy pig beside you has cooked up this little entertainment for you. But don't you worry. I fancy, by the time my guv'nor and your dad finish with him, he'll think old King Tut has got him!"

Nancy smiled again.

"I'm not worrying, Tinker," she said cheerfully. "Perhaps it is just the prince's way of acting as courier—feels that we haven't been getting enough excitement."

"Enough!" snarled Ben Ali Said. "You will sing a different tune before you are finished with. Now, listen to me.

"There has been some conversation to-day about an under-sea passage from Gibraltar to the Moroccan coast. Well, there is one, and that is the way you are both going to travel now. I have never been through it myself, but these men came across that way to-day, and they will guide us back. When you are on the other side you will learn what your fate is to be.

"I don't want any talk or any trouble. You are both going to be permitted to walk freely, but if you try any tricks you will be packed across in a way you won't like. As for you. you cursed English pig," and he glared at Tinker, "you will have the barrel of a rifle at your back the whole way. I don't want to be bothered with you, but you'll have to come along. If you try anything, the man behind you has his orders to shoot at once. I think you can understand that. Now, line up, and get ready."

With that he turned to one of the Moors and spoke a few words. The man picked up one of the lanterns that had been set on the floor, and started ahead through a small opening which forced him to bend almost double to pass. A Moor with a second lantern followed; then Nancy was pushed along, followed by another Moor. After him was Tinker, with a Moor close behind, and Tinker had no difficulty in feeling the prod-prod of the end of the rifle-barrel as he walked. Then two other Moors with lanterns stepped into place, and last of all was Ben Ali Said.

In this fashion the procession went through the low opening, and then into a wider and higher passage, which, after a few yards, began to descend at such a sharp angle that there was constant danger of slipping, and Tinker recalled with some satisfaction that Nancy was wearing broad, low-heeled shoes of the type so popular among present-day American girls.

For some time after they started that abrupt descent Tinker made no attempt to speak again to Nancy. His mind was entirely engrossed in going over the startling statements made by Prince Ben Ali Said. And somehow Tinker knew that, in those at least, the prince had not lied.

He knew enough about the legend of the subterranean passage under the Straits of Gibraltar to realise that the rough tunnel they were descending might very well be one end of such a passage. Tinker had never paid very much attention to the yarn, for he had always been sceptical of its truth; but certainly they were apparently descending into the bowels of the Rock, and if it wasn't such a tunnel, then what could it be? Prince Ben Ali Said would gain nothing by lying. On the other hand, if they were bound for the Moroccan side, then it put a very different face on the whole affair.

He knew that their absence must be noticed after a while, and he could guess that Blake would organise a very thorough and systematic search of the whole peak once he became really anxious. But Tinker knew, too, that there had been other disappearances reported, and he had never heard that any of the missing ones had ever turned up again.

If this were a passage under the sea, if it were the tunnel of old which legend said had been used by Hannibal and his armies, then it meant that someone had rediscovered it, and that their kidnapping was not the result of any plan of a day, but the culmination of a well-thought-out plot. And he did not give Prince Ben Ali Said credit for having sufficient brains to devise such a plot on his own initiative.

Now, Tinker was a regular daily reader of the newspapers, and he took an intelligent interest in current events. He had followed carefully the reports of the new trouble between the Spaniards and the Riffs, and his own reading had been illuminated by Blake's explanation of various phases of the situation in Morocco.

Like Blake, he knew that one of the most powerful chieftains among the Riffs, and one who was a ringleader in the revolt against Spanish rule, was the individual known among the Riffs as Sakr-el-Droog, a Riffian name that concealed the identity of George Marsden Plummer.

As he gazed at those fierce Moors, who, he suspected, were, in reality, Riffs, it is not surprising that his mind should dwell on Plummer, and that he should wonder if the adventurer had had any hand in the kidnapping. For if they were actually bound for the Moroccan side, then it could only be that they were going into Riff country, for certainly their kidnapping could not be due to either French or Spanish agents.

And if that were so, then Tinker knew that he must make a bid for freedom before they reached Riff country, for he had by no means forgotten his own terrible experiences some months before, when Plummer had headed the Riff mission to London. And from what Plummer had boldly said on that occasion, Tinker knew full well that he had been destined for the slave-market in the interior of the Riff country.

Therefore it is little wonder that, as his mind dwelt on Sakr-el-Droog, the lad should realise that if he failed to get clear before he was taken to the Riff zone he would be freighted through to the slave-market, where his chances of escape would be practically nil. As to what might be Nancy's fate he shuddered to think, although he was shrewd enough to guess that she might stand a chance through ransom.

How long it took them to cover the irregular descent, Tinker could only guess; but his mind was still struggling with the problem when he became aware that, while the going continued as rough as ever, the slope was less steep.

He began now to pay more attention to the tunnel, and by the light of the swinging lanterns he could see that while it was undoubtedly a natural formation, there were signs here and there in the narrower parts which seemed to show the marks of the tools of man. He was keenly interested in it, despite the precariousness of their position, for if his surmises were correct, then it meant that they were actually passing under the Straits of Gibraltar.

In places the tunnel narrowed until the walls were only a few feet apart and the roof almost touched their heads. Again, the walls dipped away into vast halls, where the roof was lost in the blackness above, and their feet sounded hollowly on the rough stone.

Now and then Tinker could make out a narrow trickle of water on the walls, and he wondered just how far above them the waters of the Mediterranean could be. He opined uneasily that they would certainly be caught like rats in a trap if the water should choose that day to break through and flood the tunnel.

But he consoled himself with the reflection that the tunnel had apparently existed since the dim ages of the past, and, unless some subterranean earthquake should occur, would probably last for centuries longer.

The way was by no means level as it would have been had the tunnel been constructed by man. It pursued an irregular course, constantly dipping down or sloping up and twisting to right and left in a most confusing manner. Now and then they would come to branch passages which seemed to lead nowhere, and which Tinker had no doubt could lure a man to his doom if he essayed to follow them.

There was an incessant whirring above their heads, to which the Moors paid no attention, and which Tinker put down to some form of bat life, and which made him feel decidedly creepy. Then, too, they were constantly disturbing huge rats, which in the wavering light of the lanterns seemed to Tinker to have only grey lids where eyes should have been.

He was positive that untold generations of living in the dark had evolved a breed of vermin in which the organ of sight had been eliminated, and he had proof of this time and again when they crashed against his legs in their mad flight, and, with squeals of fear, raced off into the darkness.

Knowing how the average girl is filled with loathing for rats and mice, Tinker could not help but admire the gallant little American girl ahead of him, for although the vermin must be continually striking against her, she had uttered not a sound. Indeed, from the first moment of starting she had marched steadily, as if they were being conducted through the catacombs of Paris or Rome, and not in reality kidnapped prisoners in the hands of a savage band of Riffs in that legendary tunnel beneath the sea.

Tinker knew the situation in which he found himself would have to be weighed very carefully. He did not know what would be done with him and Nancy once they reached the other side, but he did know that their chances of escape would be very slim once they were inside the Riff lines. He was quite shrewd enough to guess— presuming George Marsden Plummer were behind the kidnapping— that Nancy must have been seized for purposes of ransom, and he had little doubt that Caleb MacFarlane would pay almost any price to secure her safety.

On the other hand, he hadn't the faintest intention that Plummer should get away with the game if he could do anything to spoil it. And in this he knew Sexton Blake would agree.

Tinker did not fool himself that he would be held for ransom. He had had enough experience of Plummer to know that the renegade would far rather send him into the desert to the slave-market than put any price, no matter how high, upon him.

For years he had been striving to hit at Sexton Blake in a way that would really hurt, and he knew nothing could hit Blake harder than the realisation that Tinker had been hurled into that pit of misery.

On the other hand, if he should make a break for freedom in the tunnel, and, under cover of darkness, should succeed in eluding the Moors, it by no means followed that he would be able to find his way out of the place. He had a few matches with him, but no torch, and he had seen enough already to realise that to lose oneself among some of those confusing branch passages would be the easiest thing in the world.

His only hope, he opined. would be, if he made a break, to secure one of the lanterns as well, and if he could do that, douse it until he was safe, then relight it, he was willing to take a chance on winning back to the Rock. He calculated, roughly, that they must by then have covered four or five miles, and he estimated another ten or eleven must lie between that spot and where they would emerge on the other side.

He didn't think he would get much information out of Ben Ali Said, who had been stalking along in the rear uttering not a single word. But Tinker's nerve was still with him, and it was as much out of sheer bravado as anything else that he turned his head a trifle, and said:

"Am I right, prince, in thinking that Sakr-el-Droog is behind this? Don't answer if you don't want to, but it certainly looks like his work, and I'll bet anything you didn't have the brains to cook it up!"

"You can ask Sakr-el-Droog that question when you see him!" snarled the Egyptian, who, as a matter of fact, was feeling the effect of the rough journey far more than either Tinker or Nancy. "And no more talk from you," he added. The prod of the rifle-barrel in his back told Tinker that he had better desist, but he didn't mind that.

In those words of Ben Ali Said's he had read the truth, and he knew now that George Marsden Plummer was behind the affair. And, that being so, he was determined to make a break for freedom.

He could not warn Nancy. He could only let her think what she would; and he had little hope that she would realise that he was inspired to get clear in order to be of more use than he could possibly be as a prisoner.

He acted without hesitation. Pretending to stumble, Tinker managed to give a clean drop kick to the swinging lantern just ahead of him. As the glass crashed and the Moor turned with an oath, Tinker went down on one knee and swung round like a flash.

Before the Moor behind could bring the rifle down in line with his body, Tinker had him about the knees, and had brought him to the ground with a crash. Then he rolled clear, and before the others could grasp just what was happening, he had grabbed the smashed lantern, and was racing straight for the opening to a dark passage that gaped on the left.

But Prince Ben Ali Said soon saw what he was up to. He gave a scream of rage, and shouted something to the Moors. Three rifles came up at once, and a volley of bullets followed Tinker's disappearing figure. The lead struck the wall harmlessly, and the next second he was round a bend of the passage in utter and heavy blackness.

He drew up and listened. He could hear sounds of commotion beyond; then the prince shouted again, and a wavering gleam pierced the darkness as two of the Moors came to the opening of the passage. Still Tinker waited. The smashed lantern which he carried had gone out, and he hadn't any idea what lay ahead of him.

He was not keen on tackling two of the Moors, but he was counting on their thinking that he would penetrate farther than he had, and he was hoping that, as they turned the corner behind which he stood, he would be able to bring one of them down with the broken lantern, and then, settle the other.

In another few seconds the flame of the lantern showed, and the moment the Moor rounded the corner Tinker hurled the smashed lantern full at him. It caught him in the abdomen, and he went down with a grunt. The other, however, was close behind, and, as he saw his companion go down, he lifted his rifle and fired. The bullet whistled past Tinker's head, and he lunged forward, catching the man about the middle.

The latter was a powerful specimen, but he was more accustomed to shooting from the saddle than fighting in the Anglo-Saxon way, and Tinker hoped to bring him down in the first rush. One thing he knew, and that was he mustn't give the other a chance to use the rifle again. At such close quarters a hit would blow Tinker's head to pieces.

He got one leg behind the Moor's buttock, and, with a heave, had him over. They went down together, but Tinker rolled clear. He reached for the second lantern even before he was on his feet, and, turning, sped ahead into the unknown. He rounded another corner, and then he braced his feet and tried desperately to stop himself as he saw just ahead of him the sheer edge of a stone shelf that dropped into an impenetrable well of eternity just ahead.

There was not the vestige of a ledge by which he might bridge it. He knew he must stand at bay there or return, and he chose the latter course. He swung round and scrambled back from the very edge of the chasm; then, with a yell like a banshee, he charged round the bend, crashing full into another Moor who had joined in the chase.

They went down inevitably, and Tinker drove his free fist into the other's body. It doubled up the Moor, and he scrambled to his feet again.

Once more he charged ahead; but as he rounded the second bend he ran full tilt into the two pursuers he had first sent down, and, with a snarl of murderous rage, they fell upon him.

Tinker fought like a wildcat, and for a few minutes it seemed that he must still break free; but, at the very crest of his hopes, Prince Ben Ali Said came leaping along the passage, and as Tinker broke clear, he brought the butt of a heavy automatic down on the lad's skull, sending him down like a ninepin.

The Seventh Chapter.   Blake's First Move.

SEXTON BLAKE walked for nearly two hours through the narrow, sandy streets of old Tangier before he decided what he should do. It is easy enough to understand Blake's situation in regard to the demand made by Sakr-el-Droog upon Caleb MacFarlane.

Had conditions in Morocco been normal, Blake would not have hesitated to defy Plummer, and to take the risk of outwitting him. But, with the whole Riff country in a ferment, with the country practically impassable beyond Tetuan, Guamara, Alhucemas, and Melilla, he knew that if Nancy MacFarlane and Tinker had been taken beyond any one of those points there was little chance of rescuing them by ordinary means. His only chance was to use strategy.

But what strategy?

While French Morocco was quiescent enough, there was no denying the fact that the Spaniards were having an extremely bad time of it. They still held Alhucemas, it is true, and Melilla Fort was still in their hands. But the reverse at Guamara had been no small one, and Blake knew that the number of reinforcements that could be rushed up to the front from Ceuta and Tetuan was not large.

The Spanish troops would be more or less cooped up in Melilla and Alhucemas until further regiments could be brought across from Malaga, and even in Gibraltar Blake had heard reports of mutiny among the Spanish drafts there.

If it were true that the Spanish Government in Madrid had sent out an urgent call for old General Peyler, who, though well over eighty years of age, was still the best soldier they had, then Blake knew the situation was even more serious than appeared. Only two years before the Riffs had given the Spaniards a bad setback, and Blake had strong suspicions that Sakr-el-Droog was the real leader of that uprising.

But, bad as that was, it was not a patch on the present situation, and this time he knew for a fact that Plummer was the leading spirit in the revolt. On top of that, Plummer had boasted that very evening that messengers were flying across the desert, inciting all the tribes to join in a holy war against the Spaniards, and Blake knew he had not lied when he said another hundred thousand men would answer the call. A hundred thousand fanatical Moors and Bedouins! Beyond that savage ring Tinker and Nancy MacFarlane would be helpless.

That was why Blake had not felt disposed to influence Caleb

MacFarlane in his reply to Sakr-el-Droog. If the millionaire could put up the million for Riff bonds that would probably prove not to be worth the paper they were printed on, that was his business.

It was for him to decide at what price he valued his daughter's safety, and, in the absence of any contra plan for her rescue, Blake could not speak. In his mind, if Plummer played straight, then Nancy's safety would probably be assured once the money was passed over. But he knew well enough that no sum would be set on Tinker. Plummer had tried unsuccessfully in the past to put the lad in the slave market, and Blake knew his vindictive nature well enough to realise that he would not forgo the sweets of revenge if he could avoid it.

At the same time, it went sorely against the grain to recall that George Marsden Plummer had calmly stalked into Tangier and had jeered at him in the Bhanghadi Hotel. Blake's chief aim was to rescue Tinker at any cost, but it would have given him no end of satisfaction to save Nancy as well, and fool Plummer over the million ransom which he had demanded.

It was getting on for five o'clock in the morning when Blake found himself walking through the foreign quarter, and then, as he saw the lights of the massive Savoy Hotel ahead of him, he quickened his steps. He entered the big lounge, and made his way to the desk where he saw a small group of American tourists standing, discussing a short tour into the French zone, which they apparently intended to make by motor before breakfast. When they had moved off, he approached the clerk, and asked him what the chances were for getting a car to run him out to Tetuan. At the question the man threw up his hands.

"Impossible, monsieur!" he protested. "The Tetuan road is closed. It is given over to the Spanish troops moving up, and the ambulances coming down from Guamara. Unless you have a military pass, no car could get through."

Blake thought a minute; then he said:

"I heard that General Peyler was coming over to take command of the Spanish forces. Is that true, do you know?"

The clerk nodded.

"It is true," he admitted. "General Peyler has already arrived. In fact, monsieur, he is even now upstairs in his apartments having an early breakfast. He leaves for Tetuan in an hour's time."

Blake nodded, and hurried across to a desk, where he wrote out a short note in Spanish. This he placed in an envelope, which he addressed to General Peyler and marked "Urgent." Then he returned to the desk.

"General Peyler's presence here will save me the journey to Tetuan." he said. "Will you please have this sent up at once?"

The man consented to do so, and, while he waited, Blake lit a cigarette and paced restlessly up and down the lounge. It was, perhaps, a quarter of an hour later when a young man in the uniform of a captain of cavalry in the Spanish Army stepped out of the lift, and approached him.

"You are the Senor Blake?" he asked courteously, but with his gaze taking in every detail of Blake.

"I am," responded Blake. "I sent a note up to General Peyler. I can be identified by the British consul, if you wish. But what I have to say to General Peyler is of the utmost importance, and he should know it before he goes to Tetuan."

"Will you come with me, senor, please?"

With that the officer led the way to the lift, and Blake followed. They ascended to the first floor, and, after leaving the lift, walked along to the apartments which had been allotted to the distinguished general. As they entered, Blake saw an old man seated at a table in the centre of the room taking coffee and fruit, and evidently listening to the reports of half a dozen Staff officers who had come down to Tangier to meet him.

It was away back in '98, during the war between the United States and Spain, that Blake had seen General Peyler in Cuba, but even though twenty-five years had passed since then, he had no difficulty in recognising the old war-dog. He drew himself up and saluted. General Peyler lifted his hand in response, then he fixed Blake with an eagle eye.

"I have had your letter, senor," he said curtly. "I have heard of you, and that is why I have sent for you to come up. You say you have information of importance to give me?"

"Yes, general," answered Blake composedly. "I have information to give concerning Sakr-el-Droog, one of the ringleaders of the Riff revolt. This man was in Tangier last night. I saw him and talked with him, and I know something of his plans. I have personal reasons for wishing to get behind the Riff lines, and I have come to ask you, sir, to give me an open pass that will get me through the Spanish lines. When I have explained I think you will consent."

The general was frowning heavily. "Sakr-el-Droog in Tangier last night," he rasped. Then he turned to the ring of officers who were regarding Blake incredulously. "Why was I not told of this?"

"It is impossible!" they protested in chorus. "This senor must be mistaken. Sakr-el-Droog could not get through our lines."

"He not only came through your lines, but appeared openly at the Bhanghadi Hotel, where I talked with him," said Blake curtly. "After that he left on his return, entirely unmolested. If you knew nothing of it, your espionage system must be at grave fault. Shall I proceed with what I have to say, general?"

General Peyler made a sharp gesture for one of the officers to move aside. Then he beckoned to the Englishman.

"Be seated, please, Senor Blake."

Then, when Blake had obeyed, he waved his hand at the ring of Staff officers. "Back, gentlemen, please!" he ordered. "I will hear alone what Senor Blake has to say."

They backed away out of hearing, though it was plain Blake was not being regarded with any too much favour. But that worried Blake not at all, nor did it bother the old war-dog who had been called out of his retirement in the Island of Majorca to try and bring some sort of order out of the muddle and chaos into which the whole Spanish command had fallen.

For a full half-hour the two talked earnestly together. At the end of that time the general nodded his head, and laid a withered hand on Blake's shoulder.

"I will give you the pass, senor," he said. "Your plan is a daring one, but it might succeed just because of that. Sakr-el-Droog will not anticipate such a move. I wish I were able to go with you. If you succeed, you will have achieved more than a battalion could achieve. If you fail, it can do no harm, and you alone will suffer. But I wish you luck."

The general then wrote out a pass which would see Blake through any part of the Spanish zone; then he shook hands, wishing Blake luck, and a few moments later Blake was back in the street, walking briskly towards the mosque of Afgar in search of a certain man whom he wished to employ on the daring errand on which he was bound.

BY the time Sexton Blake reached the mosque of Afgar, the call of the muezzin was already being echoed and re-echoed over the sleeping city. With an incredibly rapid change from the heavy mystery of night, the day broke over the bay, and from the narrow crooked streets the faithful poured forth to prayer.

The mosque of Afgar was one of the oldest and largest of the scores of mosques in Tangier, but it was through no intention to take part in the first prayers of the day that Sexton Blake was in its vicinity. He was there to find a certain man, and, from his previous experience of Tangier, he knew he was more likely to discover him there than in any other place.

Blake entered a little coffee-shop, and ordered a cup of the beverage for which the place is famous—heavy, black coffee, distilled to a veritable essence, and very strong. But after the night he had spent, walking and pondering, it was very welcome, and by the time the crowds were coming forth from the mosques he felt greatly refreshed.

Paying for the coffee, and saluting the old coffee-seller courteously, he emerged into the open square, and sauntered across towards the front of the mosque of Afgar.

As he had anticipated, there was the usual crowd gathered at one part of the square, interested in the antics of a native, and in the crowd Blake noticed a sprinkling of British and American tourists. But it was not they who interested him. His eyes were all for the native mountebank who was entertaining the throng, and as he pushed his way through until he could see the ragged human object who stood in the centre of the far from pleasant smelling crowd, a gleam of satisfaction came into his eyes. Then he stood waiting patiently until the rather repulsive entertainment should be over.

The ragged native was doing a sort of slow dance to the tune of a reed pipe. His filthy rags were fluttering about his skinny legs, and in his eyes was a mad look which increased as the music quickened and quickened, until it had readied the crazy cadence of the dervish whirl. Round and round he flung himself in a perfect ecstasy of insane movement, then slowly the music sank and sank, until it halted abruptly in a mournful wail.

Now the mountebank paused beside a basket which he had set in the dust, and, lifting the lid, he took out a handful of small snakes.

These he clapped to his naked breast, and again began a mad dance which grew more and more repulsive each moment, until at last, with a shrill squeal of excitement, he seized one of the snakes and thrust it into his open mouth.[2]

Sexton Blake had seen the snake-eater's dance many times, both in Tangier and Cairo, but he had never succeeded in conquering the disgust with which the final act filled him. He turned his head away, and sought for a cigarette while the beastly performance continued, noticing that some of the tourists had taken themselves off precipitately, holding their hands across the body in a way that was all too significant.

The sight enabled Blake to forget what he had just seen, and as he lit his cigarette he smiled to himself. Then he turned back, and felt for a coin as the dancer ran round the circle, holding out a skinny hand for alms.

He had almost completed the round when he came to Blake. As he reached out for the coin which Blake was holding forth, his eyes lifted and encountered Blake's. For the briefest part of a second there was a flicker of something in them, but the next moment he had passed on, and turning, Blake began walking slowly across the square.

He had reached the corner opposite the mosque, and was continuing on down a narrow street that led into one of the bazaars, when there was the sound of a shuffling footstep behind him, and a few seconds later, the snake-eater who had been entertaining the crowd a few minutes before passed him. As he did so he uttered something which only Blake heard, but it was what he had been waiting for, and as the snake-eater trotted on Blake followed at a little distance. Through the bazaar he went, getting deeper and deeper into the native quarter, until at last he saw the snake-eater enter a low house half-way down a dark passage which seemed to lead nowhere, and which seemed to beat with the throb of the hidden life of the native town. But Blake entered it boldly, and as he came to the low doorway he, too, entered.

As he stepped within he saw the snake-eater bonding almost to the ground in a salaam of the most profound respect. Blake returned the salute, and seated himself upon a mat on the floor. The other clapped his hands, and a young boy entered with a tray on which were two little cups of coffee and some cigarettes. Blake helped himself,

---

[2]   Author's Note.—This snake-eating incident is fact.

and then motioned for his repulsive host to be seated.

Had any other European been present, he might have noticed that the boy had retired just behind the curtains that covered the entrance to the rear apartment, and was gazing at the Englishman with an expression almost akin to worship. But he would have found it extremely difficult to understand how the immaculate Sexton Blake was on such apparent terms of intimacy with a ragged, snake-eating dervish of Tangier.

He would have understood, however, if he had been in Tangier some five years before, when Sexton Blake, then on a visit, had jumped into the middle of a crowded street and had lifted the snake-eater's child from beneath the very hoofs of a pair of maddened horses that were careering through the bazaar. Blake himself had been slightly injured by the flying hoofs, but he had held the child clear, and from that day the mountebank had been his slave.

And that was why after his interview with General Peyler, Blake had determined to seek out the one native in Tangier whom he knew he could trust, for such a one was needed in the daring scheme he had put up to General Peyler, and which the shrewd old war-dog had approved.

Nor could Blake have picked a better man for his purpose, for he could have found no one with more knowledge of the under-life of Morocco than one of the fanatics who battened on the superstitions of the natives, as did the snake-eater and his kind.

He was an arrant humbug, as Blake well knew, but in the many conversations they had had at different times the detective had been amazed at the quaint, philosophy of the Moor, and an extraordinary bond of understanding had grown up between them, although Blake never could quite get used to the filthy part of the dance where the live snake was eaten.

For more than an hour Sexton Blake and his weird friend talked together in low tones. At first the latter was wary and nervous, even with Blake, and from time to time he kept peering out through the doorway to see that they were not overheard. But by the time Blake was ready to leave he had unloosened the other's tongue, and he departed with a fund of extraordinary information that would have seemed grotesquely unbelievable to another European.

Blake returned from the bazaar to the Bhanghadi Hotel, where he found Caleb MacFarlane taking coffee. The millionaire informed him that he had already cabled America to realise on certain securities and remit the money by cable. Blake simply said that he would remain with the other in Tangier until the business was settled, then, explaining that he had not been to bed all night, he went to his room.

That night, according to promise, a messenger came from Sakr-el-Droog, and as the millionaire had received a cable late in the afternoon, he was able to send a satisfactory message to the Riff chieftain. At Blake's suggestion, he requested Sakr-el-Droog to send a trusted man two nights later to receive the money, and the following day a brief note arrived at the hotel saying this would be done.

That same day Caleb MacFarlane received a telegram from Marseilles saying that funds, to the extent of a million, had been received for his credit, and that half this amount had been telegraphed to the Banque National in Tangier, but that, owing to the funds of that bank being insufficient to meet such a large sum, the balance was being sent that same day in French currency by aeroplane.

At ten o'clock on the second evening Sexton Blake and Caleb MacFarlane were seated in the sitting-room which they shared jointly, awaiting the arrival of the messenger from Sakr-el-Droog. In a sealed packet on the table was the ransom money, ready to be handed over. Caleb MacFarlane had been so engrossed in his own worry that he had said little to Blake about Tinker, but this evening he had been reproaching himself, and was sympathising with Blake and trying to find out what the latter proposed doing. But Blake was in a non-communicative mood. He parried most of the other's questions by some vague remark, and finally they dropped into silence.

It was just half-past ten when a white-robed Moor entered the room. He stood regarding them for a few seconds, then he stalked across and stood before the millionaire.

"The money," he said in laboured English, "is it ready?"

The American picked up the packet.

"This is it," he replied. "But what assurance have I that my daughter will be returned safely?"

The Moor evidently did not understand the words, but he got the meaning, for he thrust his hand inside his burnous and drew out two envelopes. He scrutinised these for a few moments, then he handed one to the American, and turned to Blake.

"Are you the man who is the enemy of Sakr-el-Droog?" he asked in Moorish.

Blake nodded briefly, and the Moor handed him the second envelope. While MacFarlane was reading his letter, Blake tore open the envelope and took out the single sheet of folded paper it contained. It bore a single line, and as he read it Blake's eyes grew steely, for it said: "To-morrow the brat leaves for the slave market.—SAKR-EL-DROOG."

Blake thrust the note in his pocket and glanced towards MacFarlane. The latter held out the paper he had received, and Blake read the contents, which said:

"On receipt of one million dollars, or it's equivalent in French or English currency, I guarantee to deliver to Caleb MacFarlane that amount in bonds of the Riff Republic, and also to return safely to him his daughter, who is at present in my care.

"(Signed) SAKR-EL-DROOG."

Blake passed it back.

"There seems nothing to do but take him at his word," he said briefly.

Caleb MacFarlane nodded, and, taking up the packet again handed it to the Moor.

"This is the money," he said, in a shaking voice. "When will you bring back my daughter?"

The Moor turned to Blake.

"Tell him," he said, in Moorish, "that his child will be at this hotel to-morrow night."

With that he turned and was gone. Blake translated the promise to the American, then, with a muttered excuse, he went into his bedroom. He strode swiftly to the window and out on to the balcony. There he bent over, and, taking out his cigarette case, placed a cigarette between his lips. Following that he lit a match, and, after a puff, dropped the still-burning match over the rail.

A second later a white-robed figure stole out of the courtyard, and, on reaching the street, stood by the door until the messenger from Sakr-el-Droog appeared. As the latter threw himself into the saddle of his Arab steed, the man who had emerged from the courtyard sent a shrill whistle through the night, to which the messenger paid no heed.

With a word to his steed he was off, and went flying down the sandy street on his way back to where Sakr-el-Droog awaited him. But that messenger was destined never to keep that rendezvous, for as he swung round a corner half a dozen ragged figures appeared as if by magic, and while two of them sprang for the bridle, the rest clawed at the flowing robes of the messenger, and dragged him, kicking and cursing, down into the dust.

Swiftly they bore him away, leaving the horse to its own devices; and the few natives who witnessed the scene never for a moment thought of interfering, nor did they dream for a single moment that the tall European who passed that way a few minutes later was responsible for what they had just seen occur.

As the Moor's pony drew abreast Sexton Blake, in his disguise as a Tangier beggar, sprang up and out. The pony reared high in fright. Blake's native ally clutched the horseman and dragged him from his mount. With a snort of fear the animal dashed away. (*Chapter 9.*)

The Ninth Chapter.   Reunion.

IT is as well to draw a veil over what took place in the back room of the snake-eater's hut that night. The third degree, as practised by the American police, could be likened to a mild "pink-tea" as compared to what the snake-eater and a dozen of the worst beggars and fakirs of Tangier did to that messenger of Sakr-el-Droog by the time Sexton Blake arrived on the scene it was over, and the messenger lay securely bound and gagged, while the packet of ransom money which he had carried was hidden safely in the hut until Blake should ask for it.

Sexton Blake was not the type of man to countenance the torturing of a fellow creature, no matter what his fault, unless there was absolutely no other way out, and if the situation could be solved in no other way. But on this occasion he knew that all his appeals would fall on deaf ears, and that curt note from Plummer had decided him to give the snake-eater his way.

The mountebank offered no details of what had taken place, but as Blake entered he gave him the information that was necessary for the second step in Blake's desperate attempt to save Tinker.

In that filthy hut Blake placed himself in the hands of that gang of ragged ruffians, and when, an hour or so later, the band emerged, the tallest of all looked just as filthy and ragged as any of the others.

They made their way unostentatiously to the outskirts of Tangier, where, behind a group of dingy hovels, they found a band of wiry Arab horses waiting. They mounted at once, and, with the snake-eater and Blake in the lead, the party went off at a hard gallop into the desert, heading for a spot on the coast outside the Spanish lines, where, according to the detective's guide, Sakr-el-Droog was awaiting the return of his messenger.

Some sixteen miles out, after hard riding, they ran full tilt into a Spanish patrol, but after an examination of the pass Blake had received from General Peyler, and when the amazed officer in charge had been convinced that Blake was really a European and not the filthy beggar he appeared to be, they were allowed to proceed.

The eater of snakes knew the rough country like the palm of his own dirty hand, and, once through the Spanish lines, led the way unhesitatingly through a perfect wilderness of scrub and cactus, until they heard the sound of breakers. Blake knew they must come out on the coast somewhere between Tangier and Melilla. Here their leader drew up and dismounted, the others following suit.

One man was left in charge of the horses, and, with the snake-eater still in advance and Blake close at his heels, the party set off in single file. They went ahead in a bewildering way for the better part of a quarter of an hour, then, as they topped a slight rise, they could see the glare of many fires off to the east.

"The camp of the Moors and Berbers," whispered the guide. "The camp of Sakr-el-Droog."

He started on, but came to a stop again in the dip of a ravine, which seemed smothered with cactus. A narrow path ran through it, and it was with difficulty the line followed it. Now the consumer of serpents disposed his men on either side, but before they crouched down he whispered:

"If we have been told the truth, a small party of horsemen will soon ride through here. The one in the lead will be Sakr-el-Droog. Him we must capture. The others must be unhorsed and stampeded into the cactus. Then we must get away at once. The effendi and I will attend to Sakr-el-Droog. You others must see that every other man is sent into the cactus. Now away, dogs!"

The shadowy figures sank out of sight, and then the guide showed Blake where he must kneel.

"I go now to send forth the call," he whispered. "I shall return as soon as I get the reply. Then you and I must haul down the first horseman."

Blake whispered his understanding, and a moment later the Moor had disappeared. Not long after, the weird-sounding call of a night bird could be heard some distance along the ravine. A second and a third time it went forth, then, from away to the east, came an answering call.

All Blake knew of the mountebank's return was when he heard a faint rustling in the bushes opposite him. Then heavy silence settled down, until, about ten minutes later, a medley of soft sounds came down the ravine. There was a faint hiss of warning, and, as the sounds grew nearer, Blake gathered himself for action.

Peering out, he could see something coming towards him, and as it drew almost abreast he heard his new ally click his tongue.

Blake sprang out and up, and as the Arab pony reared high in front, he and the snake-eater had clutched the horseman, and had him off his mount.

With a snort of fear the horse went dashing onwards, and then all Hades seemed to break loose as the rest of the band rose and scared the other horses into seven fits. There were half a dozen in all, and horse after horse went dashing wildly along the path; while those who had ridden them were cursing and kicking in pain where they had been thrown into the cactus on either side.

Blake and the snake-eater had wasted no time with their prisoner. They had jerked his hands behind him while he was still on the ground, and, with a few deft turns, the Moor had him secured. Then the prisoner was jerked to his feet, and at a word from the snake-eater the party started back the way they had come. As soon as they were out of the ravine they travelled more quickly, and, although they knew it would not be long before pursuit was started, they heard or saw nothing all the way to the place where the horses were waiting. Here Blake lit a match to make sure of the identity of his prisoner, and as he saw the bearded, hawk-like features of Sakr-el-Droog, he smiled sardonically.

"Why don't you call for help, Plummer?" he asked softly.

Plummer sat in silence.

Until that moment he thought he had been the victim of some tribal raid, and that a mistake had been made. But now, as he realised the truth, he fought like a madman to break free. But the barrel of a long rifle in his ribs soon caused him to desist, and when he was lifted bodily and heaved into the saddle, he made no effort to slip down.

They rode hard and fast for the Spanish lines, where Blake's pass got them through, and from there they made back for Tangier. In the little back room of the snake-eater's hut another third degree was given that night, and this time Sexton Blake was on hand to see that it should have the desired effect. And it did.

Before the dervish snake-eater and his band had finished with Sakr-el-Droog, the Hawk of the Peak was as clay in their hands, and when Blake calmly demanded that a written order be made out for the release of Tinker and Nancy MacFarlane he got it.

Blake sent a fast horseman through to the Berber camp with the order, and while they waited he wrote and despatched a note to Caleb MacFarlane, requesting him to proceed to the Savoy Hotel, and wait in the apartments of General Peyler for the return of his daughter. The millionaire was deeply mystified on receiving this note, but he obeyed, and he had already left the Bhanghadi Hotel when Sexton Blake returned in the early hours of the morning to wash and change.

Then Blake returned to the snake-eater's hut, and was sitting there drinking coffee and smoking cigarettes with his disreputable host when an automobile belonging to the Spanish Staff at Tetuan drew up in the narrow street.

In the back were Tinker and Nancy MacFarlane—the latter looking quite unfatigued and unharmed, but Tinker showing signs of having been subjected to severe treatment, which Blake knew later had been the case, and which caused him to reflect with a savage satisfaction on the fact that he had exacted payment in full from Sakr-el-Droog. The two released captives were at a loss to understand exactly what had happened, but on the way to the Savoy Blake explained briefly.

Clinging to the sides and back and front of the car were the ragged, and, it must be confessed, dirty members of the band of beggars and fakirs who had assisted Blake in his weird expedition of the night before, and when they poured up the stairs in the wake of Blake and Tinker and Nancy, the immaculate young men of General Peyler's Staff nearly had hysterics at the invasion.

The general himself was a little overwhelmed at the sight, but when they broke apart to reveal that in their midst they had Sakr-el-Droog, the Hawk of the Peak, and the man who was responsible for all the recent trials of the Spaniards in Morocco, the old war-dog didn't care in the least what they were like. He looked first at Sakr-el-Droog, then at Sexton Blake.

"Here is the man I promised you, general," said Blake cheerfully, "the Hawk of the Peak. Perhaps this time you will clip his claws for him. The last time I turned him over to Spanish justice they let him go."

Then Blake turned to where Caleb MacFarlane was embracing his daughter. He took from his pocket the bundle of ransom money which had so nearly reached Sakr-el-Droog.

"There is your money, Mr. MacFarlane." he remarked, as he laid it on the table. "I thought you might not, after all, find Riff bonds a suitable investment. And now I have a matter of my own to attend to. I fancy Mrs. MacFarlane will wish to know as soon as possible that her daughter is safe. If you can get ready soon, I think we had better start back for Gibraltar almost at once."

"I don't understand what you have done, Mr. Blake," stammered the American, "but—"

"We can talk it over later," broke in Blake. "And now, general, with your permission, I shall retire. I understand there is a reward of five hundred thousand pesos offered for the person of Sakr-el-Droog. These friends of mine"—and Blake indicated the grinning circle of mendicants— "are responsible for his capture. I hope you will see your way to dividing the reward among them."

"Why, yes, Senor Blake," answered the general. "But will you not remain and take coffee with me. I should like to have details of this capture."

"I am sorry, general, but I must ask you to excuse me. I shall, however, send you a full written report of how the capture was effected. I think you will find it interesting reading."

Then Blake saluted, and, turning, faced Plummer, who was glowering in his direction.

Blake smiled with his lips, but his eyes were hard as points of steel.

"A pretty good effort, Plummer." he said softly, "but I think it will be some time yet before you get your latest recruit to the slave market."

"I'll get you for this —soon." snarled Plummer, speaking for the first time since he had been dragged from his horse. "I shall be free again in three days, then you look out."

Blake shrugged.

"Come on, Tinker," he said. "I want to hear what you have to say before we start back for Gibraltar."

And, taking the lad affectionately by the arm, he bowed to the company in general and walked out. They left for Gibraltar within the hour.

Needless to say, the meeting between Nancy and her mother was of a most moving nature. They were able to get another boat that same evening bound for London, and, eight days later, Blake and Tinker were back in Baker Street, little the worse for their adventure, and financially richer to the tune of ten thousand pounds which Caleb MacFarlane had insisted on Blake accepting.

But a week or so later Sexton Blake found that the boast of Sakr-el-Droog had been fulfilled, for, on picking up a morning paper, he read, in the news devoted to the latest movements of the revolt in the

Riff, that Sakr-el-Droog, a Riff chieftain, had been exchanged by the Spaniards for three officers who had been taken prisoner by the Riffs.

And when he remembered that this was the second time the Spaniards had let him slip through their hands, Sexton Blake gave vent to a few forcible expressions which he rarely allowed himself to use. And it was only when the amazed Tinker read the paragraph that he understood what had upset his master.

For both Blake and Tinker knew that with George Marsden Plummer free again, the day must come when they would once more be forced to pit themselves against the criminal renegade of Scotland Yard.

THE END.

[22100 WORDS]

The Case of the SIX RUBBER BALLS.

An illicit emerald prospector wishes to smuggle his emeralds out of his country. He hides them in six balls of crude rubber. He loses them —and finds them again under tragic circumstances. His find is the beginning of a startling series of events. Sexton Blake does his bit in unravelling them—and Marie Galante (an old favourite of yours) has a hand in the affair, too. This yarn is quite up to U. J. quality. What more can you want? BETTER BOOK YOUR COPY NOW!

www.ingramcontent.com/pod-product-compliance
Lightning Source LLC
Chambersburg PA
CBHW050906120626
46554CB00003B/1035